AMAZING AMPHIBIANS

SALAMANDERS

James E. Gerholdt

Published by Abdo & Daughters, 4940 Viking Drive, Suite 622, Edina, Minnesota
55435.

Library bound edition distributed by Rockbottom Books, Pentagon Tower, P.O. Box
36036, Minneapolis, Minnesota 55435.

Printed in the United States.

Cover Photo credits: Peter Arnold
Interior Photo credits: James Gerholdt, pages 1-12, 14, 16, 17, 19
       Peter Arnold, pages 13, 15
       Barney Oldfield, page 18
Photos 4, 7, 11 courtesy of Black Hills Reptile Gardens.
Photos 8, 10 courtesy of Eric Thiss.

Edited By Bob Italia

LIBRARY OF CONGRESS CATALOGING-IN-PUBLICATION DATA

Gerholdt, James E., 1943—
 Salamanders / James E. Gerholdt.
   p. cm. -- (Amazing amphibians)
 Includes bibliographical references and index.
 ISBN 1-56239-313-8
 1. Salamanders--Juvenile literature. [1. Salamanders.] I. Title. II. Series:
 Gerholdt, James E.,   1943- Amazing amphibians.
 QL668.C2G46 1994
 597.6'6'--dc20   94-18430
                 CIP
                 AC

Contents

SALAMANDERS

Salamanders are amphibians. Amphibians are ectothermic.
This means they get their body temperature from the environment.
If they get too hot, they will die. And if they are too cool, their
bodies won't work. Salamanders need moisture to live, or they will
dry up and die. There are over 350 species found in the world.
Some salamanders are called newts. All salamanders have legs.
Most have four legs, but some species have only two. Most
salamanders have smooth skin, but some newts have bumpy skin.

The Fire salamander from Europe has smooth skin.

The Fire-bellied newt from Asia is a salamander and has bumpy skin.

SIZES

Some salamanders grow to be very large. The largest species is the Japanese giant salamander. It can grow to a length of over five feet! The Chinese giant salamander, a close relative, grows to almost four feet. In the United States, the two-toed amphiuma is the longest. It can grow to almost four feet in length, but is much more slender than the Japanese and Chinese species. Another very large species is the hellbender, which grows to a length of over two feet and is very big around. But most salamanders are much, much smaller.

The Eastern newt only grows to about four inches in length.

This Tiger salamander may grow to a length of one foot.

SHAPES

Most salamanders have long bodies with long tails and front and rear legs. But some species only have one set of legs. None of the salamanders have claws on their feet, and this makes it easy to tell them from a lizard. But some of the species, like the giant salamanders, are heavy bodied. So is the tiger salamander from the United States. Some of the species that spend their entire life in the water have bright red, feather-like gills.

The Mudpuppy spends its entire life in the water and has bright red gills.

The Chinese newt has a very long tail and legs.

COLORS

Most salamanders have colors that help them blend in with their surroundings. This is called camouflage. Most salamanders are some shade of brown or black. But some species are very brightly colored. Some species of newts are brown or black on the back, but have brightly colored bellies.

The Blue-spotted salamander from Minnesota has bright blue spots but still blends in with its surroundings.

This Fire salamander from Europe has bright colors.

HABITAT

Salamanders need moisture to live. Some species live on the land and others live in the water. The salamanders that live on the land hide under rocks or logs, and sometimes burrow deep into the ground. Others may live in trees. The species that live in the water may be found in swamps, underground caves, ponds, lakes, and rivers and streams. Some species are found in streams high in the mountains. All of the really large species are found in the water.

The Tiger salamander from Minnesota likes to hide under logs.

This Fire salamander from Europe is at home in these moss-covered rocks.

SENSES

Salamanders have the same five senses as humans. Their eyesight is good and they can see their enemies before it is too late. The species that live on the land have movable eyelids to protect the eyes. Species that live in the water do not have eyelids. Most salamanders don't make noise. But the Pacific giant salamander from the west coast of the United States may "bark," much like a small dog, if it is disturbed.

The Tiger salamander has good eyesight.

The California newt has eyes with movable eyelids.

DEFENSE

The most important defense of salamanders is their camouflage. But if they are seen by their enemies, they have other ways to protect themselves. Some species have a sticky slime that comes from their skin. It can glue the mouth of an enemy shut while the salamander escapes. Brightly colored species can kill an enemy with their bad taste! Some of these species will lash out with their tail or hold the tail in the air so that the bad taste can protect them.

The Chinese newt tastes bad and may lash out at an enemy with its tail.

16

The Chinese newt blends in with its surroundings.

FOOD

All salamanders eat other animals. Most species eat things like insects, spiders, slugs, snails and worms. But some of the larger species will eat anything they can fit into their mouth. Their tongue is used to help moisten the food and move it in the mouth. A few species can flick the tongue out to catch their food, just like a frog or toad. Other species lunge forward and grab their food.

An Eastern newt is eating an earthworm.

This Tiger salamander is enjoying a tasty king mealworm.

BABIES

Salamanders have their babies in more than one way. Many species lay their eggs in the water. Then these hatch into larva which metamorph (or change) into the adult form and leave the water. Other species lay their eggs on the land, under rocks or logs. These hatch into tiny salamanders which look like adults. A few species keep the eggs in their body while they develop and give birth to tiny young. The number of young or eggs can be from less than 20 to 500. Some species guard the eggs until they hatch.

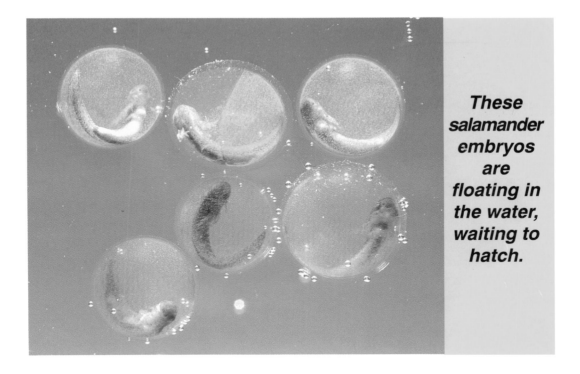

These salamander embryos are floating in the water, waiting to hatch.

This Marbled salamander is guarding its eggs.

GLOSSARY

Amphibians (am-FIB-i-ans)-Scaleless animals with backbones that need moisture to live.

Camouflage (KAM-oh-flaj)-The ability to blend in with the surroundings.

Ectothermic (ek-toe-THER-mik)-Regulating body temperature from an outside source.

Environment (en-VI-ron-ment)-Surroundings an animal lives in.

Habitat (HAB-e-tat)-A place where an animal or plant lives.

Larva (LAR-va)-A newly hatched amphibian.

Metamorph (MET-a-morf)-To change from a larval to an adult form.

Index

About the Author

Jim Gerholdt has been studying reptiles and amphibians for more than 40 years. He has presented lectures and displays throughout the state of Minnesota for 9 years. He is a founding member of the Minnesota Herpetological Society and is active in conservation issues involving reptiles and amphibians in India and Aruba, as well as Minnesota.

Photo by Tim Judy